Ten fat sausages, sizzling in a pan.

One went POP and the other went BANG.

Now there's eight fat sausages, sizzling in a pan.

Eight fat sausages, sizzling in a pan.

One went POP and the other went BANG.

Now there's six fat sausages, sizzling in a pan.

Six fat sausages, sizzling in a pan.

One went POP and the other went BANG.

Now there's four fat sausages, sizzling in a pan . . .

Now it's time to meet a new pan of sausages
with ideas of their own . . .

To Callum and Lily xx —M.R.

For my super studio mates,
silly sausages all! —T.F.

···INGREDIENTS···

W

PENGUIN WORKSHOP
An Imprint of Penguin Random House LLC, New York

Penguin supports copyright. Copyright fuels creativity, encourages diverse voices,
promotes free speech, and creates a vibrant culture. Thank you for buying an
authorized edition of this book and for complying with copyright laws by not
reproducing, scanning, or distributing any part of it in any form without permission.
You are supporting writers and allowing Penguin to continue to publish
books for every reader.

Text copyright © 2018 by Michelle Robinson. Illustrations copyright © 2018 by
Tor Freeman. All rights reserved. First published in the United Kingdom in 2018 by
Andersen Press Ltd. Published in the United States in 2020 by Penguin Workshop,
an imprint of Penguin Random House LLC, New York. PENGUIN and
PENGUIN WORKSHOP are trademarks of Penguin Books Ltd, and the
W colophon is a registered trademark of Penguin Random House LLC.
Manufactured in China.

Visit us online at www.penguinrandomhouse.com.

Library of Congress Cataloging-in-Publication Data is available upon request.

ISBN 9781524793296   10 9 8 7 6 5 4 3 2 1

Ten fat sausages, sizzling in a pan.
One went POP and the other went . . . .

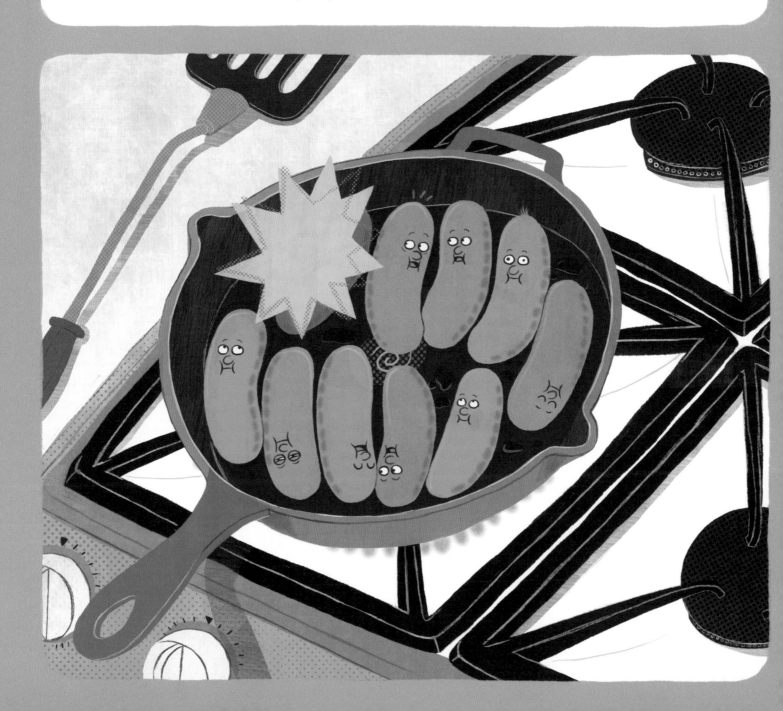

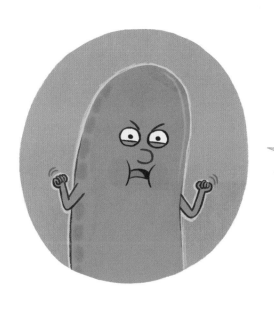

Hang on a minute!
I do not like this.
The fridge went hummm,
but the pan goes hissss.
Well, I won't go BANG
and I won't go POP.

And Sausage Number Two went hop, hop, hop.

Over the counter and glug, glug, glug!

He was doing quite well till they pulled out the plug.

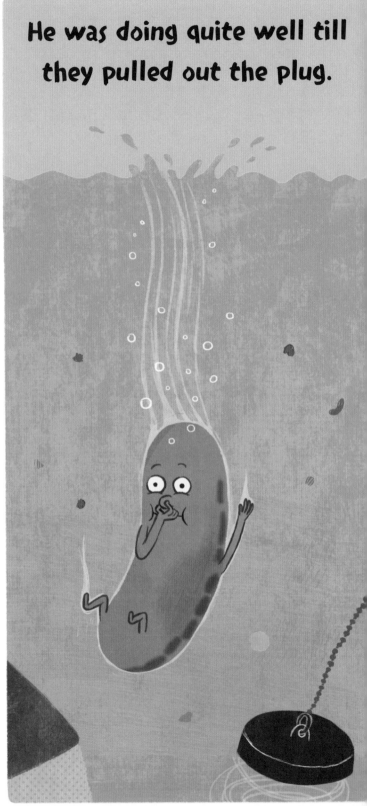

He spluttered and reached for the chain.
But Sausage Number Two
WHOOSHED straight down the drain.

Eight fat sausages, sizzling in a pan.
One went POP and the other went . . .

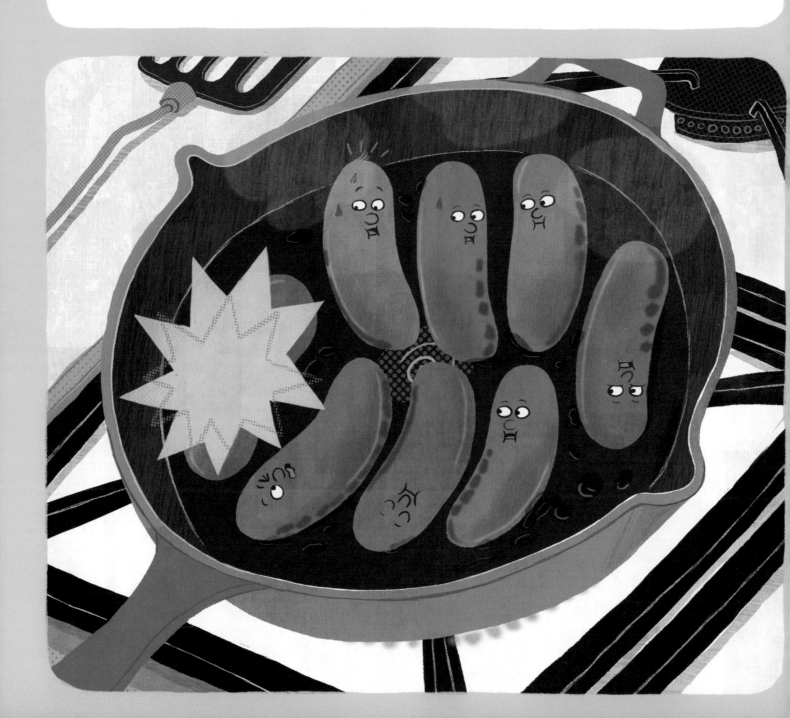

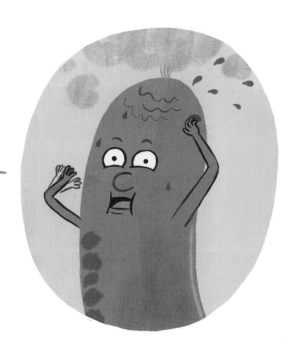

HANG on a minute! I've had quite enough of sitting around in this hot, oily stuff. Well, I won't go BANG and I won't go POP.

And Sausage Number Four went hop, hop, hop.

Over the counter
and into a bowl.
"This is much more
comfortable."

"Yes, on the whole
I am far better off.
But this switch is a mystery . . .

Six fat sausages, sizzling in a pan.
One went POP and the other went . . .

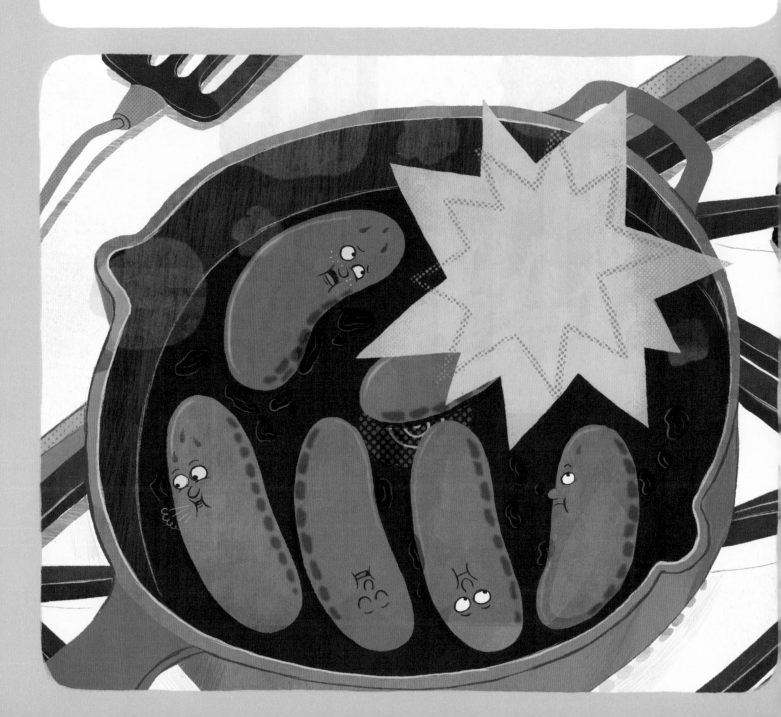

HANG on a minute,
I want to escape!
I don't want to end up
on somebody's plate.
Well, I won't go BANG
and I won't go POP.

And Sausage Number Six went hop, hop, hop.

Straight up the cookbooks
and onto the fridge.

Over the wide-open Freezer Top Ridge.

"The whole world awaits,
I'm a freewheeling man.
GIDDYAP!"
Sausage Six was
flung by the fan.

Four fat sausages, sizzling in a pan.
One went POP and the other went . . .

HANG on a minute, that was my best friend. She didn't deserve such a terrible end. Well, I won't go BANG and I won't go POP.

And Sausage Number Eight went hop, hop, hop.

Down from the counter and over the floor.

Past the cat's bed.
"If I just reach the door . . ."

Two fat sausages, sizzling in a pan.
"Try not to POP. We'll escape—I've a plan . . ."

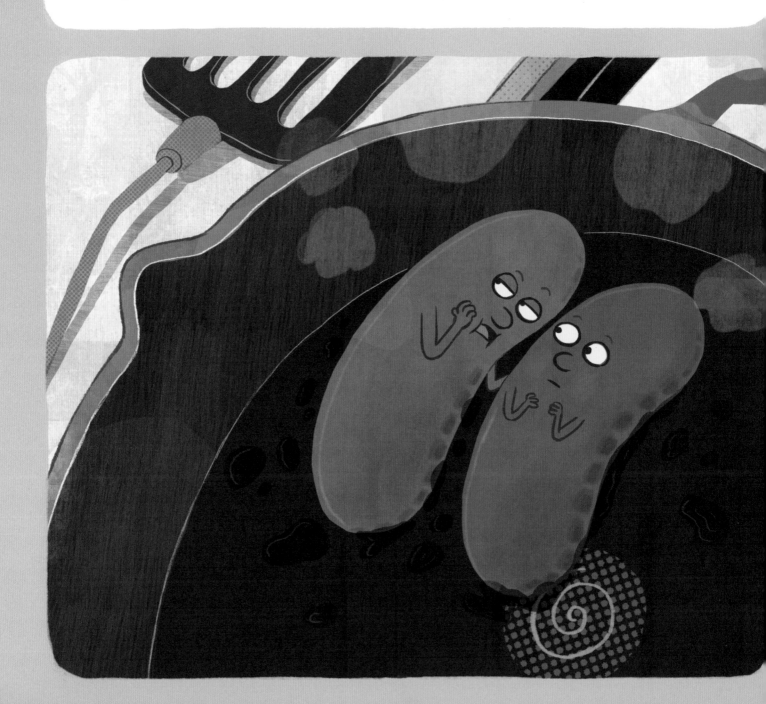

BANG!

yelled the sausage,
and

POP!

said his brother.

The stove was switched off.
They embraced one another.
Now, as sausages go,
that last plan was quite clever.
Might this pair survive?

Over the counter they went at a run.
"Let's hide in this squishy thing. Whee! This is fun!"
They hulaed in onion rings, danced in red sauce.
Two silly sausages . . .